A NOTE TO PARENTS

Congratulations on choosing the best ~~educational~~ materials for your child. By selecting our top-qua~~lity~~ products, you can be assured that the concepts used in our books will reinforce and enhance the skills that are being taught in classrooms nationwide.

And what better way to get young readers excited than with Mercer Mayer's Little Critter, a character loved by children everywhere? Our First Readers offer simple and engaging stories about Little Critter that children can read on their own. Each level incorporates reading skills, colorful illustrations, and challenging activities.

Level 1 – The stories are simple and use repetitive language. Illustrations are highly supportive.
Level 2 - The stories begin to grow in complexity. Language is still repetitive, but it is mixed with more challenging vocabulary.
Level 3 - The stories are more complex. Sentences are longer and more varied.

To help your child make the most of this book, look at the first few pictures in the story and discuss what is happening. Ask your child to predict where the story is going. Then, once your child has read the story, have him or her review the word list and do the activities. This will reinforce vocabulary words from the story and build reading comprehension.

You are your child's first and most influential teacher. No one knows your child the way you do. Tailor your time together to reinforce a newly acquired skill or to overcome a temporary stumbling block. Praise your child's progress and ideas, take delight in his or her imagination, and most of all, enjoy your time together!

Library of Congress Cataloging-in-Publication Data

Mayer, Mercer, 1943-
The new fire truck/by Mercer Mayer.
    p.cm. -- (First readers, skills and practice)
"Level 2, Grades K-1."
Summary: Little Critter and his classmates come up with ideas to earn money for the fire department's new fire truck.
ISBN 1-57768-843-0 (pb : alk. Paper)
[1. Moneymaking projects–Fiction. 2. Fire engines–Fiction. 3. Schools–Fiction.] I. Title. II. Series.
PZ7.M462 Ng 2003
[E]—dc21   2002008755

Gingham Dog Press
An imprint of Carson-Dellosa Publishing LLC
P.O. Box 35665
Greensboro, NC 27425 USA

Printed in Rockaway, NJ USA • All rights reserved.   ISBN 1-57768-843-0

4 5 6 7 8 9 10 PHXBK 15 14 13 12 11 10   201107791

FIRST READERS

Level 2   Grades K–1

THE NEW
FIRE TRUCK

by Mercer Mayer

GINGHAM DOG
P R E S S

An imprint of Carson-Dellosa Publishing LLC
Greensboro, North Carolina

One day Miss Kitty gave our class
a special project.
We're going to raise money
for a new fire truck.

We washed cars.
Tiger and I rinsed off the soap
with a big hose.

7

8

We had a bake sale.
I brought brownies that I baked
with just a little help from my mom.

We set up a lemonade stand.
I squeezed the lemons.

11

We walked dogs.
Gabby and I walked Fluffy together.

Our whole class gave the money
we raised to the fire department.
They said soon they would bring
us a big surprise.

The fire department came to our school.
They brought the surprise.

16

It was the new fire truck.
What a great class project!

Word List

Read each word in the lists below. Then, find each word in the story. Now, make up a new sentence using the word. Say your sentence out loud.

Words I Know
truck
washed
soap
walked
school

Challenge Words
special
money
squeezed
together
department

Periods in Abbreviations

Some words can be made shorter.
These words are called abbreviations.
These abbreviations end with a
period. Days of the week can
be abbreviated.

Example: Sunday ——→ Sun.

Point to the correct abbreviation for each day
of the week.

Monday   ——→ Mon   or   Mon.

Tuesday   ——→ Tue   or   Tues.

Wednesday   ——→ Wed.   or   Wednes.

Thursday   ——→ Thurs   or   Thurs.

Friday   ——→ Fri.   or   fri.

Saturday   ——→ Satur.   or   Sat.

A Visit to the Fire Station

Look at the picture on the next page.
Then, point to three things that start with the
same sound you hear at the beginning of bell.

Next, point to three things that start with the
same sound you hear at the beginning of sun.

Finally, point to three things that start with the
same sound you hear at the beginning of horse.

21

Story Parts

Every story has a beginning, a middle, and an end.

At the beginning of the story, Miss Kitty gave the class a project. What was the project?

In the middle of the story, the class did different activities to raise money. Name three of the four activities.

What other fundraising activities could they have tried?

Finally, what happened at the end of the story?

Why do you think it took a few months for the end of the story to happen?

R Blends

All three of the words below start with an r blend. To say these words, blend the sound of the first letter with the sound of r.

Examples: Friday   brought   project

In each row below, point to the picture or pictures that begin with the same sound you hear at the beginning of the first picture.

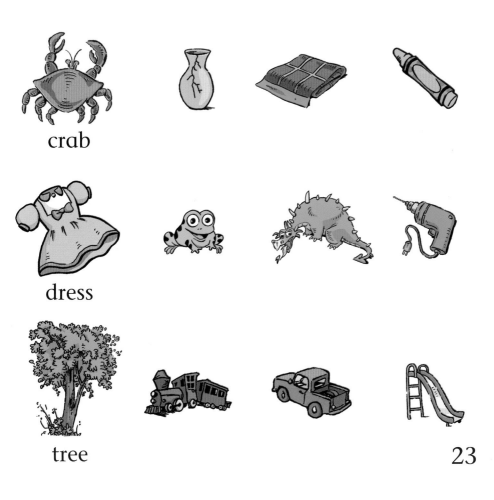

crab

dress

tree

Answer Key

page 19
Periods in Abbreviations

Monday → Mon or (Mon.)

Tuesday → Tue or (Tues.)

Wednesday → (Wed.) or Wednes.

Thursday → Thurs or (Thurs.)

Friday → (Fri.) or fri.

Saturday → Satur. or (Sat.)

page 20
A Visit to the Fire Station

Answers will vary: badge, backpack, buttons, bucket, boy, boots

Answers will vary: soap, seven, sponge, spots, siren

Answers will vary: helmet, hose, heart, handle

page 22
Story Parts

What was the project?
To help raise money for a new fire truck.

Name three fundraising activities
washed cars, had a bake sale, set up a lemonade stand, walked dogs

What other fundraisers could they have tried?
Answers will vary.

What happened at the end of the story?
The fire department brought the new fire truck to school.

Why do you think it took a few months for this to happen?
They probably had to order it, wait for it to be delivered, etc. Answers will vary.

page 23
R Blends

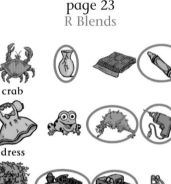

crab

dress

tree